MY  GOLDFISH

BARROUX

EERDMANS BOOKS FOR YOUNG READERS
Grand Rapids, Michigan ● Cambridge, U.K.

My goldfish
is the strongest goldfish
in the world.

When someone bullies him,
my goldfish can defend himself on his own.
He is afraid of nothing.

If there is one thing my goldfish hates, though, it's fighting.

For Halloween,
my goldfish loves to dress up
and scare everybody.

At night, sometimes
my goldfish has nightmares.
But if I sing softly to him,
he falls back to sleep.

I've told him a hundred times
not to speak to strangers,
but my goldfish
never listens.

My goldfish
has a beautiful voice.
When he sings,
the whole world listens.

Every time my goldfish goes on vacation,
it's the same old story:
he comes back sunburned.

They say that goldfish
don't have a good memory.
Mine often forgets where he lives.

On Saturday mornings,
my goldfish swims laps at the local pool.
When he comes back,
his eyes are all red.

For the last few days,
my goldfish has been acting very strange . . .
I think he's in love.

I have to change the fishbowl
water every day.
My goldfish really lives like a pig.

If you give lots of love to a goldfish,
he can live a very, very, very long time.
Mine is already 110 years old.

I know that one day, though,
when he's really too old,
my goldfish will jump out of the bowl and leave.

He will finally swim with the great white fish.

Barroux has worked as an art director, a magazine illustrator, and a children's book author and illustrator. His work has appeared in such publications as the *New York Times*, the *Washington Post*, *Forbes*, and the *Wall Street Journal*. His recent books for children include *Where's Mary's Hat?* and *Mr. Katapat's Incredible Adventures* (both Viking). Barroux lives in France.

© 2006 Éditions Nathan (Paris, France)

This edition published in 2009 by agreement with Éditions Nathan by
Eerdmans Books for Young Readers
an imprint of Wm. B. Eerdmans Publishing Co.
2140 Oak Industrial Dr. NE, Grand Rapids, Michigan 49505
P.O. Box 163, Cambridge CB3 9PU U.K.

www.eerdmans.com/youngreaders

Manufactured in Singapore

09 10 11 12 13 14 15   8 7 6 5 4 3 2 1

Library of Congress Cataloging-in-Publication Data

Barroux, Stéphane.
[Mon poisson rouge. English]
My goldfish / written and illustrated by Barroux.
p. cm.
Summary: The proud owner of an extraordinary goldfish describes its amazing talents.
ISBN 978-0-8028-5334-9 (alk. paper)
[1. Goldfish — Fiction. 2. Fishes — Fiction. 3. Pets — Fiction.] I. Title.
PZ7.B275675My 2009
[E] — dc22
2008009999